BAD
DOGS

CHARLES GHIGNA

ILLUSTRATED BY
DAVID CATROW

Hyperion Books for Children

FIRST EDITION
1   3   5   7   9   10   8   6   4   2
Library of Congress Catalog Card Number: 92-52985
ISBN: 1-56282-290-X / 1-56282-291-8 (lib. bdg.)

Dogs jump fences,
dogs give chase,

dogs lick neighbors
in the face.

Dogs chew flowers,

dogs dig holes,

dogs knock over
doggy bowls.

Dogs like bushes,
dogs like trees,

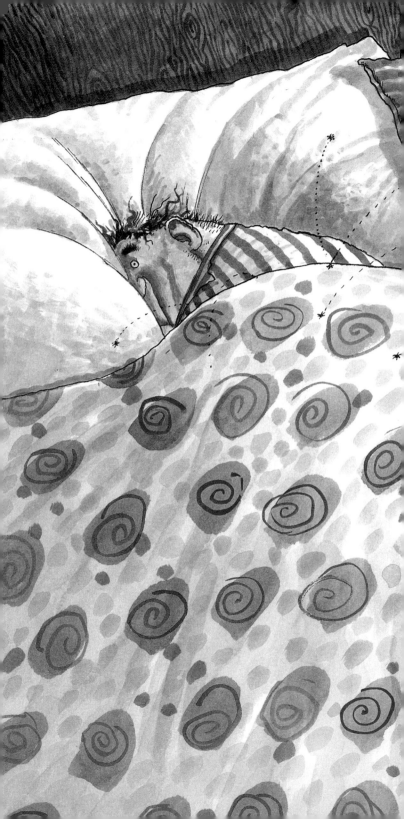

dogs like sharing
all their fleas.

Dogs are frisky,
dogs forget,

dogs are friendly
when they're wet.

TO SEE THE
OTHER SIDE OF

DOGS,

FLIP THIS BOOK
TO START AT THE
BEGINNING.

TO SEE THE
OTHER SIDE OF
DOGS,
FLIP THIS BOOK
TO START AT THE
BEGINNING.

dogs are always
man's best friend.

Dogs are loyal,
dogs defend,

dogs can sometimes
shake your hand.

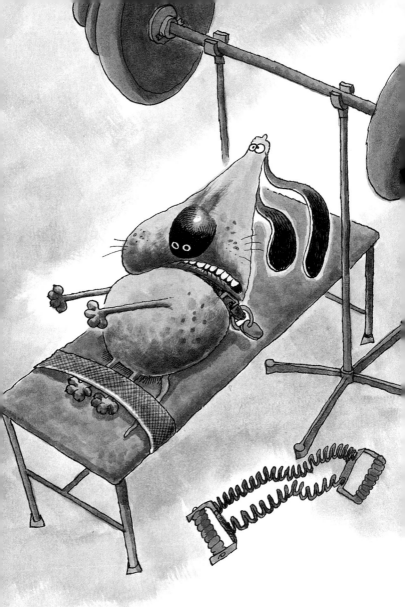

Dogs can sit up,
dogs can stand,

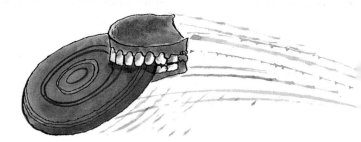

dogs catch Frisbees,
dogs fetch sticks.

SKIDMORE C LLEGE LIBRARY

Dogs do dog shows,
dogs do tricks,

dogs are bashful,
dogs are bright.

Dogs are docile,
dogs delight,

FIRST EDITION
1 3 5 7 9 10 8 6 4 2
Library of Congress Catalog Card Number: 92-52985
ISBN: 1-56282-290-X / 1-56282-291-8 (lib. bdg.)

Good DOGS

CHARLES GHIGNA

ILLUSTRATED BY
DAVID CATROW

Hyperion Books for Children